Puppy Friends™ #6

Billy the Brave Puppy

by Jenny Dale
Illustrated by Frank Rodgers

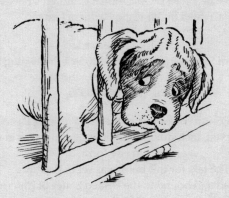

Aladdin Paperbacks
New York London Toronto Sydney Singapore

Look for these Puppy Friends books!

#1 *Gus the Greedy Puppy*
#2 *Lily the Lost Puppy*
#3 *Spot the Sporty Puppy*
#4 *Lenny the Lazy Puppy*
#5 *Max the Muddy Puppy*

Coming soon:

#7 *Nipper the Noisy Puppy*

Special thanks to Narinder Dharmi

First Aladdin Paperbacks edition October 2000
Text copyright © 1999 by Working Partners Limited
Illustrations copyright © 1999 by Frank Rodgers
First published 1999 by Macmillan Children's Books U.K.
Created by Working Partners Limited

Aladdin Paperbacks
An imprint of Simon & Schuster Children's Publishing Division
1230 Avenue of the Americas
New York, NY 10020

The text for this book was set in Palatino.
Printed and bound in the United States of America

2 4 6 8 10 9 7 5 3 1

Library of Congress Catalog Card Number: 00-106716
ISBN 0-689-83554-X

Chapter One

"Look, Billy, this is your new home!"

Billy looked up nervously at Martin, his new owner.

Martin put the brown and white puppy down on the living room carpet and smiled at him. "You're going to live with us now!"

Billy glanced around the strange

room. Everything looked different. Everything *smelled* different. And worst of all, his mom wasn't here.

Billy and his five brothers and sisters had lived with their mother in Mrs. MacDonald's house, where they had been born. But seven dogs were more than the MacDonalds could care for, so when the puppies were a few weeks old they'd started going away to new homes. One by one, Billy's brothers and sisters had left with their new owners until only Billy was left. No one had picked Billy because he always ran off to hide when strangers arrived. Then Martin had come to visit.

That day, Billy burrowed his head under the blanket in his mom's basket, hoping no one would notice him. But soon he felt a hand stroking his back. He'd been spotted!

A friendly voice said, "Hi, Billy. Will you come out and say hello to me?"

Billy peeked his head out from under the blanket and gave the boy's hand a quick lick.

But now, that friendly boy had brought Billy to a strange new home. He didn't like it one bit! His stubby little tail drooped, and he began to whimper.

"He seems frightened, Dad," Martin said in a worried voice.

"Well, it'll take him a little while to settle in," Mr. Newman replied. "After all, this is the first time he's been away from his mom."

Feeling miserable, Billy stared up at Martin and Mr. Newman. He wished he was back at Mrs. MacDonald's house, snuggled up safely with his mom in their basket.

Martin kneeled down and held out his hand. "It's all right, boy," he said.

"No one's going to hurt you."

Billy pushed his nose into Martin's hand. Even though everything was strange and scary, he did feel safe with Martin. "At least *you* smell nice and friendly!" he snuffled.

Martin laughed. "That tickles!" he cried, and he began to tickle Billy's fat tummy.

Billy rolled over onto his back, wagging his tail. "This is fun!" he yelped. He was beginning to feel much better.

Ding-dong!

Billy nearly jumped right out of his skin. He bounded across the room on his big, clumsy paws and dived behind the sofa.

"It's all right, Billy!" Martin hurried over to him. "It's just the doorbell, that's all."

Billy stayed behind the sofa. He knew what a doorbell was. It meant that someone was waiting outside. But this doorbell was much louder than Mrs. MacDonald's, and Billy didn't like it.

Martin's mom popped her head around the living room door. "It's the window cleaner," she said. Then she glanced around. "Where's Billy?"

"Hiding!" replied Martin's dad with a smile. "I don't think he likes the doorbell!"

Martin bent down and looked into the darkness behind the sofa. All he could see were two big, brown eyes looking back at him. "Come on out, Billy," he said gently. "It's okay, boy."

But Billy didn't move. He didn't know what a window cleaner was, and he wasn't taking any chances.

"I don't think Billy believes you, Martin!" said Mrs. Newman with a grin.

Martin tried again to coax his puppy out. "Come on, boy. There's nothing to be scared of."

Billy liked Martin and didn't want to disappoint him. He crawled along the carpet on his tummy until his nose was just peeking out.

"Good boy!" said Martin, scratching the top of Billy's head. "See? Everything's okay."

But as Billy wriggled out of his hiding place, he spotted a huge man outside the living room window—and he was throwing water at them! Billy yelped and disappeared behind the sofa again, bumping his head on the wall as he went.

"Billy, it's just the window cleaner!" Martin called.

But Billy backed farther away behind

the sofa. There had never been any strange men throwing water at the windows of Mrs. MacDonald's house!

Martin's dad laughed. "He's not exactly the bravest puppy in the world, is he?"

"He'll be all right when he's settled in," Martin said, defending his puppy. "I know he will."

"I hope so," said Mr. Newman. "He's going to be a big dog when he's fully grown. In a few weeks, he won't be able to fit behind the sofa anymore!"

Martin looked behind the sofa again and noticed a small puddle next to Billy. "Uh-oh . . . can you get a paper towel, please, Dad? Billy's had a little accident!"

Mr. Newman grinned and went off toward the kitchen.

Behind the sofa, Billy was feeling rather embarrassed.

"Billy?" Martin said softly. "Come on out, boy. I won't let anyone hurt you."

Billy looked at Martin and decided to trust him. Making a big effort, he crawled slowly to the edge of the sofa again and peeked out. The strange man had gone. Billy wriggled out quickly and dashed up to Martin.

"Good boy!" Martin picked up the puppy and hugged him. Then, holding Billy close, Martin whispered, "I know just what it's like to feel scared, Billy."

Billy licked Martin's chin. "It's horrible, isn't it?" he sniffed.

"There's a bully at school named Jamie Jones who keeps coming after me," Martin confided.

Billy didn't know what a bully was, but it didn't sound very nice.

Martin buried his face in Billy's short, thick coat. "I'm really scared of him. He takes all my lunch money."

Just then, Mr. Newman came in with a wet cloth to wipe up Billy's puddle.

Billy pretended not to notice and busied himself licking one of Martin's ears. The puppy liked Martin and his mom and dad. Perhaps living here wouldn't be so bad after all.

Chapter Two

"Time for bed, Billy." Martin picked up the puppy and carried him over to the brand-new dog basket in a corner of the kitchen.

Billy yawned. It had been a long, exciting day.

"This is one of my old blankets," Martin said, tucking a cozy blue blanket around the puppy. "It's yours now."

Billy snuggled in, but something wasn't right. Surely he wasn't supposed to sleep here in this strange basket, all on his own?

Martin stroked Billy's head. "Sleep well, boy. See you in the morning." And he went out, turning off the light.

The kitchen was very dark without the light on. Billy began to imagine all kinds of horrible creatures lurking in the shadows, waiting to get him.

He sat up and whimpered. He'd never had to sleep on his own in the dark before. Even when all his brothers and sisters had gone, he'd still had his mom to snuggle up to every night.

Billy's ears went down, and he began to howl.

"Billy! What's the matter?" Mr. and Mrs. Newman both rushed into the kitchen, followed by Martin in his pajamas.

Billy clambered out of his basket, skidded across the slippery kitchen floor, and flung himself at Martin's legs.

"I don't like the dark!" he whimpered.

"I think he's scared, Mom," Martin said, picking up the shivering puppy. "Can he sleep upstairs with me?"

"Well, all right," Mrs. Newman said reluctantly. "Otherwise none of us are going to get any sleep. Take his basket with you."

A few minutes later, Billy was tucked up in his basket again. But this time he was right next to Martin's bed. Although the room was dark, Billy could hear Martin close by, snoring softly. Now he didn't feel scared at all.

"It's all right, Billy." Martin bent down and looked behind the TV. "You can come out now. It was only Mrs. Simpson from next door."

"Well, okay, if you're sure!" Billy whimpered. He slowly crept out and then jumped up at Martin for a reassuring pat.

It was the following morning, and Billy had rushed to hide as soon as he heard the doorbell. He wondered if he was *ever* going to get used to all the strange sounds and smells in his new home.

"Come on, Martin, time to go to school," called Mrs. Newman. *School?* Billy thought. *What's that?*

"Bye, Billy." Martin kneeled down and gave Billy a hug. "I wish I could stay here with you! I'll see you tonight."

"But I want to go with you, Martin!" Billy whined. "I want to go to school, too, whatever that is!"

"Martin, you're going to be late," his mom warned him as she came into the room, dragging a vacuum cleaner behind her.

"Oh, no! Not a vacuum cleaner!" Billy yelped. He just couldn't understand why people liked pushing them over the floor so much. As far as Billy could see, they didn't really do anything except make a horrible loud noise that made his ears hurt.

He rushed off to hide.

"Billy, watch the lamp!" Martin shouted. But it was already too late. One of Billy's big paws had caught in the lamp's cord, and it was toppling off the shelf.

Martin rushed across the room and caught the lamp as it fell.

"Sorry!" Billy yelped. He rushed off in another direction, saw the rug in front of the fireplace, and burrowed his way out of sight.

Martin and his mom couldn't help laughing.

"I don't think Billy likes vacuum cleaners, Mom!" Martin said. "Maybe he'd better go out into the backyard."

That seemed like an excellent idea to Billy. He dashed out of the room. Then he skidded to a halt in the hallway. He

couldn't remember where the backyard was.

"This way, Billy." Martin led Billy into the kitchen and unlocked the back door.

Oh, that's right, Billy thought, wagging his tail. *I remember now.* Martin had taken him out to play yesterday, before it got dark.

Billy ran out onto the lawn. "Come on, Martin! Let's play!"

"Sorry, boy," Martin said as he walked down the path. "I have to go. See you later." He went through the back gate, closing it carefully behind him, and walked off down the street.

Billy poked his head through the gate and watched Martin disappear around the corner. Then he sat down on the grass. Why did Martin have to go to school?

"Martin should be back from school soon," Mrs. Newman told Billy at last.

"Good!" Billy woofed. He could hardly wait for Martin to get back. He

had been gone for ages!

Billy liked Mrs. Newman. Earlier when Billy had been hungry, Mrs. Newman had given him some food and a cuddle. She was very kind. But Billy had more fun with Martin.

"I'll let you out into the backyard, Billy," Mrs. Newman said. "You can watch out for Martin coming down the road." She opened the back door.

Billy scampered through the yard to the gate and poked his head out. As he watched, Martin came running around the corner. "Great!" he yelped. "Martin's coming back to play!"

Martin was running very fast, as if he couldn't wait to get home. Billy wagged his tail happily.

But then his tail went still. Something was wrong. Martin looked scared!

Suddenly a big, fierce-looking boy came around the corner, chasing after Martin. He was shouting loudly.

Billy didn't understand what the boy was saying—and he didn't want to, either. It was all too frightening. He had to hide!

The puppy saw a large bush near the gate. He rushed over and squeezed behind it. There were lots of sharp twigs sticking into him, but at least he was out of sight.

He heard Martin's feet thundering up to the gate and hurrying through it. The gate slammed shut again. He could hear Martin panting hard, but he couldn't hear the other boy. Quickly, Billy scrambled out from behind the bush and ran up to Martin.

"Hi, boy." Martin dropped his backpack and bent down to pick up Billy. "Were you waiting for me?"

"Yes, I was," Billy sniffed. He still felt a little worried. "Has that big, scary boy left?" He peered over Martin's shoulder to look out into the street.

The road looked empty again. Relieved, Billy licked Martin's cheek.

"Did you see that boy who was chasing me?" Martin whispered. "That was Jamie Jones. He's a real bully. I barely

got away from him this time!"

"What a horrible boy!" Billy yapped indignantly. So a bully was someone who chased you and shouted at you and scared you to pieces. Billy had guessed that bullies weren't very nice, and he had been right!

Billy felt very sorry for Martin. And he couldn't help feeling a little ashamed, too. When Martin was in trouble, Billy had hidden behind a bush instead of helping. Billy whined miserably. "Oh, I wish I was brave."

Chapter Three

"Come on, Billy!" Martin called, picking up his puppy's leash. "Let's go for a walk."

Billy was delighted. It was the weekend again. Billy had been at his new home for two weeks now. He knew that the weekend meant two whole days with Martin!

"It's Mom's birthday tomorrow, Billy," Martin said as they went out through the back gate.

Billy tried to look as if he knew what Martin meant, but he wasn't quite sure what a birthday was.

"I'm going to buy her a big box of chocolates," Martin told him.

Billy was still puzzled. He didn't know what chocolates were, either.

There were some shops two streets away, next to Martin's school. Martin was allowed to go there on his own because there were no busy roads to cross.

Billy enjoyed going for walks with Martin. He only took Billy to the park or down quiet streets where there weren't many loud cars and trucks, and he always picked Billy up if a bigger dog came along. Billy felt very safe with him.

"Here we are, boy." Martin led Billy up to one of the shops and stopped outside the door. "I can't take you in with me, so you'll have to wait here."

"Oh, do I *have* to?" Billy whined as Martin tied his leash to a nearby fence. "*Why* can't I come with you?"

"I won't be long," Martin promised, patting Billy on the head.

Billy watched Martin walk into the shop. He huddled against the fence, trying not to be noticed. Billy hated being left alone in the street. He tried to tell himself that there was really nothing to be frightened of.

And then he saw Jamie Jones, the bully!

For a moment, Billy couldn't believe his eyes. Jamie Jones was walking down the street, straight toward him!

Billy sat there, still as a statue, as the big boy came closer. What if Martin came out of the shop and walked right into him?

But to Billy's relief, Jamie Jones walked right past the shop Martin was in and went into the one next door.

Just then Martin came out holding a shopping bag.

"Thank goodness!" Billy panted,

leaping up at Martin. "We've got to leave—right now!"

"All right, calm down, boy!" Martin laughed. "Look what I've got!" He opened the shopping bag and took out the big box of chocolates he'd bought. But Billy was in too much of a hurry to take a look.

"Quick, Martin!" he yapped urgently.

"We've got to get out of here!"

"I got something for you, too, boy," Martin said with a grin. He pulled out a small bag. "Doggy Chocolates!"

Billy gave the bag a quick sniff to be polite, then yelped, "Thanks very much—but please, get a move on!"

"Hey, calm down, Billy," Martin gasped as the puppy pulled hard on his leash, "or you won't get a treat."

"I don't *want* a treat!" Billy whined. "I want to get out of here before Jamie Jones comes out of that shop next door!"

"I guess you want your breakfast," Martin said, untying Billy's leash and winding it firmly around his hand. "Okay, we'll save the treats for later."

As Martin led him away, Billy looked anxiously at the door of the shop Jamie Jones had gone into. Luckily, there was no sign of him. Billy stopped pulling so hard on his leash. They'd soon be safely back home again.

Then Billy's heart sank as Martin stopped outside another shop, saying, "I need to buy some wrapping paper here."

"All right," Billy whimpered nervously. "But hurry up!"

As Billy watched, Jamie Jones came out and walked off in the opposite direction, toward the park. Relieved, Billy flopped down on the pavement.

But then Billy got another shock.

Instead of going home the way they had come, Martin began to lead the puppy toward the park.

"No!" Billy yelped, sitting down on the pavement. "We can't go that way!"

"Are you tired, Billy?" Martin asked. "Do you want me to carry you?"

"No!" Billy yelped again. He jumped to his feet and tried to pull Martin in the other direction. "We've got to keep away from that horrible boy!"

Martin shook his head and pulled the puppy back. "If we go this way, we can cut through the park. You'd like that, wouldn't you?"

Billy had to give in. But he walked as slowly as he could, hoping that by the

time they reached the park, Jamie Jones
would be miles away.

"At this rate it'll be lunchtime when
we get home," Martin sighed, tugging at
the leash. "Come on, Billy!"

At last they arrived at the park. It was
still early, and the park was empty—
except for one boy, sitting on a swing,

looking bored. It was Jamie Jones.

Billy froze, the hairs on the back of his neck standing up all stiff and bristly. As soon as the bully saw Martin and Billy, he jumped off the swing and came toward them with a big grin on his face.

His heart pounding with fear, Billy stared up at Martin. "What are we going to do *now?*" he whined softly.

Chapter Four

"Well, look who it is—Martin Newman," Jamie Jones said with a nasty grin.

Billy tried to hide behind Martin's leg, his head and tail down.

The bully swaggered up to Martin and Billy, trying to look cool, his baseball cap on backward. A strong gust of wind blew the cap right off, and Jamie had to run and grab it. He glared at Martin and Billy as if it were *their* fault, then jammed the cap back on his head.

"So, Newman, are you going to run away from me again, you little coward?"

Martin had to clear his throat before he could speak. Even then he could hardly get the words out. "I—didn't run away from you," he stammered.

"Oh, yes, you did." Jamie Jones reached out and poked Martin in the chest with a stubby finger. "I don't like cowards!" His voice was so loud that Billy nearly jumped out of his skin.

Billy crept closer to Martin. He looked desperately up and down the park, hoping that maybe some grown-up would come past and stop Jamie Jones from bullying them. But there was no one else around.

"Is that your dog?" Jamie Jones asked, glancing scornfully at Billy. "He looks like a real wimp!"

Billy backed away behind Martin's legs, trying to make himself as small

as possible. He didn't know what a wimp was, but he guessed it wasn't a compliment.

"If I had a dog, I'd have a rottweiler," Jamie said boastfully. "Something really fierce—not a stupid little dog like that!"

"Billy's not stupid!" Martin said. This time, his voice was loud and strong.

Billy's tail gave a little wag. He was pleased that Martin was brave enough to stick up for him.

But now Jamie Jones was glaring at them again. "Got any money?" he snapped.

"No," Martin answered, his voice quiet again. "I've spent it all."

Jamie looked very annoyed. "What

have you spent it on?"

"I had to buy my mom a birthday present," Martin explained.

Jamie took a couple of steps forward until he was standing right in front of Martin, nose to nose. Billy couldn't help whimpering a little.

"Okay, have you got any candy, then?" Jamie demanded loudly.

"No," Martin muttered, holding the bag with his mom's chocolates even tighter.

"I'm starving!" Jamie grumbled. "Haven't you got *anything*?" He looked at the shopping bag. "What's in there?"

Billy's heart sank.

"Nothing," Martin said, and he put

the bag firmly behind his back. Billy knew that the chocolates were a special present for Mrs. Newman. But maybe Martin should just hand them over. Then Jamie Jones might leave them alone.

"Give me that bag!" Jamie demanded. He lunged forward to try and grab it.

Scared, Billy and Martin both jumped backward out of his way, and Jamie's foot caught in Billy's leash. He tripped, landing flat on his face in front of them.

"Owww!" Jamie roared furiously as his nose hit the ground.

"Quick, Billy!" Martin gasped, yanking frantically at Billy's leash. "Run!"

Billy and Martin raced off down the path, with the puppy funning faster than he'd ever run in his life. He didn't even dare to look back to see if the bully was following them.

When they got to the park gates, Martin stopped and looked back over his shoulder. Billy took a quick look, too, his heart pounding nervously. But there was no sign of Jamie Jones.

"I think we got away from him, Billy!" Martin said, panting. He grinned shakily. "Did you see the look on Jamie's face when he tripped? It was so funny!"

"Serves him right!" Billy yapped.

Martin scooped Billy into his arms

and gave him a hug. "Don't worry, boy, we'll be home soon."

Billy could hardly wait. He just wanted to have his breakfast, then go to sleep in front of the fireplace. He'd had enough excitement for one day!

They walked through the streets. As they got close to home, Billy began to feel much better.

Then, as they passed the huge old oak tree on the corner of Martin and Billy's street, someone jumped out right in front of them. It was Jamie Jones.

"Thought you got away from me, huh?" Jamie said, smiling nastily. "Well, you didn't. I ran through the park and got here first!"

Martin and Billy stared at him, too surprised to move.

"Okay." Jamie held out his hand. "You better show me what's in that bag or else!"

Slowly, Martin opened the shopping bag.

Jamie looked inside, and a big grin split his round face. "Chocolates! Great!"

"They're for my mom's birthday," Martin said desperately.

But Jamie Jones didn't care.

"Hand them over!" he ordered.

Chapter Five

Billy couldn't bear it. How *dare* Jamie Jones make Martin so frightened and unhappy? He just *had* to be stopped!

As Jamie reached out to grab the chocolates, a strange thing happened to Billy. A weird feeling bubbled up from his tummy and through his chest. It came out of his mouth as a sound he'd heard other dogs make.

"*Grrr . . . Ruff!*"

Jamie Jones dropped the chocolates and jumped nervously away from Billy.

Martin stared down at Billy in surprise. He'd never heard his puppy *bark* before.

Billy was surprised himself. He hadn't even known that he *could* bark! And not only that—his bark seemed to have scared horrible Jamie Jones!

Billy looked at Jamie and decided to try out his bark again. "*Grrruff . . . ruff ruff . . . RUFF RUFF RUFF!* Not so brave now, are you!" he barked. He strained at the leash as if he was desperate to get free and show the big bully a thing or two!

Jamie Jones leaped backward, his baseball cap falling off onto the pavement. "Keep that dog away from me!" he yelled.

Martin shook his head, trying to hide a smile. "You've annoyed Billy now, Jamie," he said. "He can be very tough when he needs to be!"

Jamie wailed and rushed behind the tree again.

"You'd better leave us alone, or I'll take him off his leash!" Martin called, bending down as if he was about to set Billy free.

"Okay, okay! I'll leave you alone—I

promise!" Jamie cried. "Just call off your dog!" Then he ran up the road at top speed, leaving his baseball cap on the ground.

Martin burst out laughing and swept Billy up into his arms. "Good job, Billy! You were so brave!" he said, hugging his puppy close.

"Me? Brave?" Billy woofed, in between licking Martin's face all over. "Well, I guess I was, a little bit."

Billy felt very proud of himself. Even though he'd been scared stiff, he'd stuck up for Martin. And now he really did feel braver. He felt so brave, he could have burst!

"*Ruff ruff RUFF!*" he barked.

"Let's go home, boy." Martin gave the puppy a final cuddle and put him back on the ground. "I don't think Jamie Jones will be bothering us anymore, thanks to you!"

Billy trotted proudly down the street with his head held high. A car zoomed noisily past them, and he didn't even care. Then a man walked by with a Labrador retriever on a leash. But this time, Billy looked the big dog straight in the eye as they passed each other.

"You don't scare me!" Billy woofed confidently. After all, he was Billy the *brave* puppy now, wasn't he?

When Martin and Billy got home, Mrs. Newman came to the door to let them in.

"Oh, Martin, you'd better put Billy in the backyard," she said. "I'm just about to vacuum the hall."

"Yes, you'd better make yourself scarce, Billy," remarked Martin's dad as he came down the stairs. "We don't want any more accidents!"

"I'm not scared of that noisy old thing anymore!" Billy barked.

Martin's mom and dad looked at Billy in surprise. "He barked!" they said together.

Martin nodded. He grinned as Billy trotted down the hall and sat right next to the vacuum cleaner. "I don't think Billy's scared of anything anymore, Mom," he said.

Mrs. Newman shook her head. "But Billy's scared of *everything!*" she replied. "Just watch. . . ." She switched on the vacuum cleaner, and it began to roar.

But Billy just blinked lazily, yawned, and stayed where he was.

"Well!" Mrs. Newman switched the machine off again. "I don't believe it."

"Neither do I!" added Mr. Newman.

"I told you," Martin laughed. "Billy's really brave now."

Billy sat up and barked proudly.

"I don't think I'll do the vacuuming after all," Mrs. Newman muttered, looking dazed. "I think I need a cup of tea after a shock like that!"

"Good idea," agreed Martin's dad, and they both went off to the kitchen.

"Oh, I almost forgot," Martin said, digging in his shopping bag. He took out the bag of dog treats, shook one into his hand, and offered it to Billy. "Here you are, boy. Try this."

Billy sniffed the treat. It smelled okay. . . . He wolfed it down. It was delicious. "May I have more treats?" he woofed hopefully.

Martin gave him another one. And another. And *another!*

"Thanks, Billy," he whispered. "If it weren't for you, I'd still be getting

bullied by Jamie Jones."

In between treats, Billy woofed and gave his owner a lick. "If it weren't for you, Martin, I'd still be scared of *everything!* But from now on, we can be brave together!"

Everyone loves Kitten Friends!

Meet Felix the Fluffy Kitten from
Kitten Friends #1

"Oh, they're all adorable!" Jodie said as five tiny kittens played around her feet. There were three fluffy gray kittens, like their mother, and two sweet black-and-white ones with pink noses.

Jodie sighed deeply. "I'm never going to be able to choose!" She got down on the floor and picked up one kitten at a time. "Oh, I don't know!" she wailed.

Jodie's mom smiled. "Can you help, Mrs. Dent?"

"They're all good, clean little kittens," Mrs. Dent said. "But the short-haired black-and-whites would be easier to care for. The gray kittens, being long-haired, will need lots more grooming."

"Oh, I won't mind doing that," Jodie said. "I will love combing my kitten." She held up one of the gray fluffies. "This one has the bluest eyes. And he's really fluffy!"

The kitten looked at Jodie and meowed, "Choose me!"

Everyone needs Kitten Friends!

Fluffy and fun, purry and huggable, what could be more perfect than a kitten?

by
Jenny Dale

#1 Felix the Fluffy Kitten
0-689-84108-6 $3.99

#2 Bob the Bouncy Kitten
0-689-84109-4 $3.99

#3 Star the Snowy Kitten
0-689-84110-8 $3.99

#4 Nell the Naughty Kitten
0-689-84029-2 $3.99

#5 Leo the Lucky Kitten
0-689-84030-6 $3.99

#6 Patch the Perfect Kitten
0-689-84031-4 $3.99

ALADDIN PAPERBACKS
Simon & Schuster Children's Publishing
www.SimonSaysKids.com

Everyone needs Puppy Friends!

Bouncy and cute, furry and huggable, what could be more perfect than a puppy?

by
Jenny Dale

#1 Gus the Greedy Puppy
0-689-83423-3 $3.99

#2 Lily the Lost Puppy
0-689-83404-7 $3.99

#3 Spot the Sporty Puppy
0-689-83424-1 $3.99

#4 Lenny the Lazy Puppy
0-689-83552-3 $3.99

#5 Max the Muddy Puppy
0-689-83553-1 $3.99

#6 Billy the Brave Puppy
0-689-83554-X $3.99

#7 Nipper the Noisy Puppy
0-689-83974-X $3.99

ALADDIN PAPERBACKS
Simon & Schuster Children's Publishing
www.SimonSaysKids.com